In a Cloud of Dust

Alma Fullerton

art by Brian Deines

pajamapress

First published in the United States in 2015

www.pajamapress.ca   info@pajamapress.ca

  Canada Council   Conseil des arts   ONTARIO ARTS COUNCIL   Canadä
for the Arts   du Canada   CONSEIL DES ARTS DE L'ONTARIO

The publisher gratefully acknowledges the support of the Canada Council for the Arts and the Ontario Arts Council for its publishing program. We acknowledge the financial support of the Government of Canada through the Canada Book Fund (CBF) for our publishing activities.

Library and Archives Canada Cataloguing in Publication

Fullerton, Alma, author
        In a cloud of dust / Alma Fullerton ; art by Brian Deines.
ISBN 978-1-927485-62-0 (bound)
        I. Deines, Brian, illustrator II. Title.
PS8611.U45I52 2015   jC813'.6   C2014-906879-4

Publisher Cataloging-in-Publication Data (U.S.)

Fullerton, Alma, 1969-
    In a cloud of dust / Alma Fullerton ; art by Brian Deines.
[32] pages : color illustrations ;   cm.
Summary: A Tanzanian schoolgirl struggles with a long walk to and from school that leaves her no daylight in which to do homework. When studying at lunchtime makes her miss out on the bicycle library's visit, her compassionate classmates find a way to share the bicycles so that everyone can reach home.

ISBN-13: 1-978-1-927485-62-0
1. Tanzania – Juvenile fiction. 2. Friendship – Juvenile fiction. 3. School children – Tanzania – Juvenile fiction. I. Deines, Brian, 1955- . II. Title
[E] dc23   PZ7.F8454In 2015

Cover and book design by Martin Gould
Original art created with oil paints on canvas

Manufactured by Sheck Wah Tong Printing Ltd.
Printed in Hong Kong, China

Pajama Press Inc.
181 Carlaw Ave. Suite 207 Toronto, Ontario Canada, M4M 2S1

Distributed in Canada by UTP Distribution
5201 Dufferin Street Toronto, Ontario Canada, M3H 5T8

Distributed in the U.S. by Ingram Publisher Services
1 Ingram Blvd. La Vergne, TN 37086, USA

For my dad, who taught me how to ride a bike
and always stayed close by to catch me if I fell
— A.F.

For Anne
— B.D.

In a Tanzanian village,
a little schoolhouse sits
at the end of a dusty road.

During lunch break, Anna works inside.
There will be no daylight for schoolwork
by the time she reaches home.

In a cloud of dust,
a pickup screeches to a stop,
interrupting a football match.

From the doorway,
her teacher calls,
"Anna, come outside."

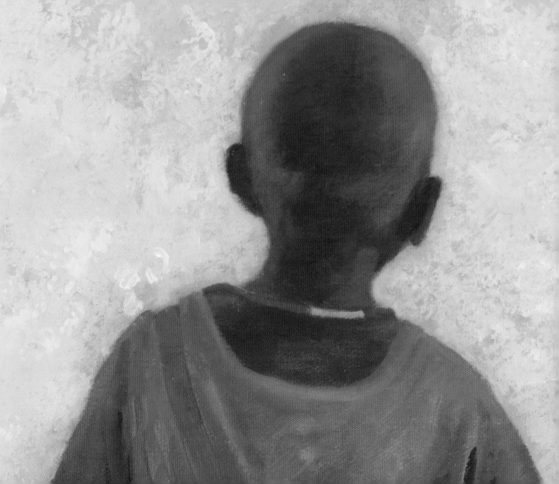

As the dust outside settles,
Anna sees the sign on the truck,
BICYCLE LIBRARY,
and Joseph, from the bicycle repair shop,
unloads bikes.

Irene spies the perfect bike.
Mohammad digs a bike from the pile.
And Farida uncovers one just right for her.

By the time she gets there,
Anna is too late
and the bikes are gone.

Anna is disappointed
but she's excited to help her friends.

Anna teaches Leyla to balance.

She directs Samwel
around the obstacles

Left

Right

Stop!

And she encourages Prisca
when she falls.

After school,
Anna's journey home
takes much less time.

Anna runs
beside Farida.

She bumpety-bumps
with Samwel.

She helps
Leyla careen.

She twists and turns
with Irene.

Down the hill,
Mohammad brakes
at his stop.

When they get off the bike,
Mohammad hands it to Anna.
"You have farther to go."

Anna calls, "I'll pick you up tomorrow!"

Past the golden wheat,
over a pot-filled trail
and down a narrow path
toward home,
Anna kicks up her own
cloud of dust.

Author's Note:

In Tanzania and other parts of Africa, cars, aircraft and other vehicles are found everywhere; but there are still millions of people who can't afford those luxuries. About 50% of people in the southern African countries are what their governments consider 'stranded' (with no access to any motorized transportation) or 'survival' (with very limited access to motorized transportation). Bicycles are vital to such communities. Not only do bicycles help many of these people get to their jobs and schools, they also create jobs for people through sales, bike repairs, and libraries.

In many of these 'stranded' or 'survival' communities, children have to walk several hours to and from school. Their families can't always afford to buy bicycles. Organizations like the Village Bicycle Project and Bikes for Humanity donate bicycles or have opened bicycle libraries all over Africa, where a child can sign out a bicycle just like we sign out books at our libraries.

It is estimated that there are about 15 million functional bicycles in existence in the southern African countries, but only about 30% of those are used for transport or commuting by adults and children. So there is still a great need for more bikes for these communities.

Here is a list of some organizations that distribute bikes to Africa and other developing countries.

BICYCLES FOR HUMANITY, CANADA.
www.bicycles-for-humanity.org

B4H has 50 chapters in 5 countries. To date, 80 Bicycle Empowerment Centers have been created in 8 countries. Since 2005, more than 75,000 bikes have been shipped to developing countries.

BIKES ACROSS BORDERS, Austin TX
bikesacrossborders@riseup.net;
www.facebook.com/BikesAcrossBorders

Bikes Across Borders has organized more than ten bike delivery caravans since 2001, sending over 500 bicycles to Cuba, Mexico, and Central America.

BIKES FOR THE WORLD, Washington DC.
www.bikesfortheworld.org

For the past 7 years, Bikes for the World has been the largest, on an annual basis, of the international bicycle recycling organizations and is building a national movement to collect and distribute second-hand bicycles for productive use. Since beginning in 2005, it has delivered more than 90,000 bicycles to programs serving low-income individuals and their communities across the globe. In 2013, Bikes for the World delivered 13,650 bicycles to more than a dozen selected service organizations, focusing on Africa and Central America, but with significant numbers going to the Philippines and community groups in the eastern U.S.

VILLAGE BICYCLE PROJECT,
Seattle WA and Moscow ID USA.
www.villagebicycleproject.org

Village Bicycle Project collects and ships used bicycles and develops bicycle training programs in Ghana. The project also provides specialized bicycle tools to bike repairers. They've also done some work teaching girls to ride in Sierra Leone.

WORLD BICYCLE RELIEF, IL USA.
www.worldbicyclerelief.org

World Bicycle Relief manufactures and distributes new bicycles on a large scale and for a reasonable price to charitable projects in Kenya, Zambia and Zimbabwe.

WORLDBIKE, Oakland, CA.
http://worldbike.org

This organization distributes cargo bikes.